7OVE ETERNA7

7OVE
ETERNA7

AXEL R. CRISTALES

7ove Eterna7

First Edition

ISBN: 979-8-4894-1373-2

FOR MY MUSE

I hope, when you read these words, that you're reminded of the one who loved you. Thank you for always believing in me. These are your words as much as they are mine.

ARC

7ove Eterna7 is a collection of poetry and prose about love found, love lost, and the in-between moments and emotions that make love worth living and dying and living for again. Each writing consists of seventy-seven words.

TABLE OF CONTENTS

There is no easy way from the earth to the stars.

- Seneca

IN THE BEGINNING

A thought rested in my mind, a feeling lurked in my heart, a destiny dreamt in my soul, a desire treaded on my skin. And like magic, déjà vu, you appeared; when you looked at me and I looked at you every verse and lyric I'd memorized as a child suddenly made sense. It was a crossroads moment where minds, hearts, souls, and bodies collided. It was the beginning of a story more eternal than the universe.

BETWEEN SHADOW AND SOUL

Night and day, gentle winds blow. Silently. Invisibly. In their wake, flames are fanned, desires deepened. In my universe, you are both cause and effect of the fire continuing to defy and define my darkness. You are where I find the moon. You are where I find the sun. Alone in the cold, I've learned that you can't set a heart on fire without casting shadows. And you can't fall in love without casting away your soul.

THE ETERNAL THREE

I. Faith

Faith, please forgive me. You wanted to meet halfway. You looked at me and said, "Come. I am here for you." I looked the other way and ran, too afraid to see myself the way you saw me. I couldn't fathom why your beauty would open its arms to me. Now, I feel lost and breathless; I am drowning amongst broken dreams. But then, suddenly, I feel a hand reaching for me. Faith, I know it's you.

II. Hope

Hope, please don't pass me by. I have endured restless nights since turning my back on you. Whatever light once shone through my window, the rays now appear obscure.
"God," I pray.
"Look within your heart," He answers.
I close my eyes. I see you smiling. Hope, in you I find my grace. I'm broken, but you make it feel okay. And even if it isn't, I'm certain that one day you'll make sense of it all.

III. Love

Love, my soul wastes away, empty without you. Where does meaning come from if not from you? You teach that the important thing is not what you get, but what you give. Love, you make the poor man rich and the lame man run. You are slow to take and quick to share. Wherever I go, you are there. Wherever lost, however long, faith and hope will guide, and you will sustain. Love, you help me persevere.

BEAUTIFUL PARADOX

Love is discovering heaven and hell with another, knowing that nothing is easy, yet everything is simpler when you go through it together. Love is the black and white keys on a piano. Played individually, it's just noise. Played together and you can dance carelessly to music in the rain. Love is the beginning of the end, because you realize that there was no life before her and that, after her, there will never be life again.

CONTENTMENT

I talk. You listen.
You talk. I feel you.
I cry. You give me your shoulder.
You cry. I give you my heart.
I say, "I'm scared." You say, "I'm here."
You say, "I'm scared." I say, "I've got you."
I say, "Life sucks." You say, "Baby, YOU make it good."
You say, "Life is good." I say, "Beautiful, YOU make it great."
I love. You love.
You love. I love.
We toast. We drink. To us.

A THRU Z

love **A**wakens
and pushes us **B**eyond life's limits
love **C**ompels us
to set the worl**D**
ablaz**E**
Frees us
to i**G**nite
lig**H**t in darkness
love **I**s
the **J**ourney and destination
toward a **K**indred
sou**L**
Moving us
to climb mou**N**tains
l**O**ve is
the **P**ower with which we
con**Q**uer
fea**R**

and de**S**pair
Through love we reach the moon
and disting**U**ish the other side
lo**V**e is
Why we endure the climb
before the ape**X**
love is its own discoverY
the **Z**enith

MAY I HAVE THIS DANCE

"May I have this dance?" I took your hand and asked, though I had no idea how and without a compass to guide me.
What I had was a feeling, leading me towards you.
How could you have known I couldn't dance? I moved clumsily, stepping on your feet, and holding you more closely than was required.
You smiled at me and said, "I like you."
Right then, I knew I had found my forever dance partner.

M-YOU-SIC

There is a bridge that always brings us together. Me in the distance and you waiting somewhere in time. Yet the crossover occurs when I play our songs. The road bends, the road is obstructed, but the direction is unfailing when I push play. In the sublime, my emotions match a current, not knowing whether I'm coming or going, only knowing that I'm being taken somewhere with you. Music, a love language only the soul can interpret.

FEEL ME

Feel you, upon awakening and imagining your smile
while the sunrise kisses me good morning.
Feel you, under the midday sun as the winds blow by,
your sweet scent intimating former desire.
Feel you, as the sun goes down and night slowly
approaches, embracing the feeling of past and present
fulfillment.
Feel you, as the stars light my bedroom with echoes
and shadows of minds being blown, occupying the
distance between us.
Feel me? I feel you.

THE UNDENIABLE

There are lies that, because of fear, become reality. There are tears that, because of pride, become smiles. There is pain that, because of mercy, becomes pleasure. There may be falsehoods that might cover the truth, but they will never undo the truth. For the truth, like the sun, cannot be denied. It sets and rises without justification. It casts shadows yet cannot be shadowed. You are the sun I can't conceal, my truth I can't deny.

US, BABY

The world sees us how it wants to see us. The world pretends and points its fingers. And to the world we throw two back—deuces. For we stay true to one another, and that's where we find our peace. Our love is unafraid, unapologetic. It takes no prisoners. In life's battlefield, you're my flag and I'm your soldier. We ride and die side by side. We're all we need. It's us against the world. Us, Baby.

INKED

You tagged me. I was your canvas. You were the artist holding a palette full of colors. You were gentle. It was painless and liberating. Marks were left in the throes of attraction and affection. I'm now a display of your artistry. Though some tattoos carry more ink than others, all are permanent. But none are more permanent, none are more beautiful, than the images inked by the one whose needle penetrates the heart, body, and soul.

MIDNIGHT SUN

It is will against will, a place between the known and the unknown. It is the dark night of the soul. In the silence of my soul, a voice calls to you. In the shadows of the night, a voice calls to them. My heart, much like a flower, thrives in the light. Without you, it will wither and die. And what light through yonder window breaks? As darkness paints the horizon, you are my midnight sun.

WINTER ROSE

Dusk ushers in the desolation and darkness. The
warmth once felt is now gone.
"Don't ever forget," I hear a voice echo across the
barren valley.
Dormant grass and snow crinkles underneath my
feet as I march in search of the voice. The wandering
makes me weary. I stop and rest.
"You are not alone," the voice whispers.
I strike a match and a red rose appears before me. I lie
next to it and fall asleep.

BOTTLES AND SHOTS

Let me drink from every bottle I see and take shots with all who care to toast with me. "To you, my Winter Rose! For you, my Midnight Sun!"
May my suffering tonight come not from this vice, but from all thoughts of you. You deliciously torment me and slowly drive me crazy. I sip on your memory; you go down smooth. While the liquor gets me buzzed, it is still you that makes me weak. ¡Salud!

LOVE OF MY LIFE

In darkness, I always find you. You're a shining path. Even if I never see you again, my soul will forever be guided by your light. My soul which, in the loneliness of dawn, kisses you good morning and, in the solitude of dusk, kisses you goodnight. Even if you never come back to me, you'll forever be the love of my life, because, regardless of where life takes me, you'll be the one I always seek.

IMAGINING

I love imagining what it will be like next time we meet. I know not the place, nor time, nor under what circumstances. I don't know if it'll be in this life or in the next. I don't know in what form we'll meet again, but I'm certain we will. As moon and night, rain and earth, sun and flower, leaves and autumn, we are destined to meet again. And I just love imagining when and where.

#1

I could have a million followers. Thousands of stars could fall to my left, kneel to my right. Hundreds of beautiful women could walk past me, and I'd be left wondering and thinking about you. For my reality is this: in the end, it all comes down to the one that the universe is pulling me towards. Only one can make sense of it all. In the end, you are that one. The only one I want.

TEACHER APPRECIATION

Dear Miss J,

Thank you for teaching me there are more than twenty-four hours in a day. Thank you for modeling how one plus one can still equal one. Thank you for showing me true chemistry. Thank you for helping me understand that reason sometimes has no reason, and for teaching me a new language. Thank you, Miss J, because you taught me all there was to know about love except how to forget.

Your student,
ARC

YOUBIQUITY

I try to ignore, yet you are there at the airport as I scan the list of cities under departures.

You are there when I play a song I can't stop singing along to. You are there every time I look down at my watch, wondering, "is time an enemy or an ally?" You are there in the excitement and stillness of days and nights. Why ignore, when you've already made every place I try inhabiting yours?

ONE WAY FLIGHT

I want to fly to a place where only you know my name, where I can wake up and know that I've arrived, with you by my side. I want us to walk barefoot on the beach, write messages in the sand, then find a cantina where we can drink until there is no remembrance of what once was while serenading you with a strolling mariachi. I want to go there with you and never come back.

PILLOW TALK

Breath subsides. Pulse slows. Your head nestles on my chest. I run my fingers through your mussed, wispy hair.
"Hey you," I whisper.
"Hi, baby," you say in a voice that matches your eyes.
"Should I put the candles out?"
"Let them burn."
"And the music?"
"Can you sing to me in Spanish?"
"Okay," I chuckle. *Voy a apagar la luz para pensar en ti, y asi...*
I nudge you. You've fallen asleep. I kiss you goodnight.

ALL OF YOUR LIGHTS

Your glittering smile
Your sparkling eyes
Your glowing hair
Your fiery walk
Your shimmering style
Your brilliant touch
Your dazzling fragrance
Your scintillating mind
Your kindling caress
Your flaming self-respect
Your incandescent heart
You lit my soul on fire while blazing a new trail in my life. Now the path left to travel illuminates with rays of you. In my constellation, you'll forever be the brightest of stars, the one that neither day nor night ever sets.

MOONBEAMS AND DREAMS

After the bottles are consumed and the world has said farewell, my mind is quelled. Moonbeams and dreams. I stagger out the door, look up, and focus. Through the starry sky, past the night's pale queen, I see you as my eyes become full of you.
Moonbeams and dreams.
I stumble to bed and drift off to sleep. Before I do, I whisper these last words: "Please God, may she feel my love tonight."
Moonbeams and dreams.

SHOOTING STAR

Goodnight, my beloved. Under the same moon, the same sky, you sleep, and with eyes closed I see you. I fixate on you, knowing that you dream while my hand caresses your peaceful face. How marvelous it is to have you near me! In the dark, I whisper, and fill the air with your words. I hold you tight, believing that, upon waking up, I'll be that much closer to you. Star light, star bright. I wish.

SLOW KISS

The sun sets. I take your face in my hands. We close our eyes. Gently, I kiss the corners of your mouth and my lips glide subtly in between, covering every millimeter of your mouth. Slowly, I slide my tongue inside. It finds yours and gently rubs against it. Ignition. Like wind fanning the flames, I breathe softly into your mouth, your lips fluttering, fire crackling within. Blaze. We pull away, open our eyes. The sun rises.

RHYTHM

I pull you in and whisper in your ear, "It's our song." Your beautiful eyes catch the lights twirling above. "Ready?" I ask.
You say nothing as you grab my hand and place it on your hip while my other hand finds yours. Fingers entwined; we dance in perfect symmetry. Wherever I go, you go. And wherever you move, I move. The music stops, but we continue as the floor empties. For love is its own DJ.

SIT AND JUST LOVE ME

"I don't know what's happening," you said in a panic as you grabbed your chest.
"What should I do?" I asked, searching for your other hand.
A tear tracked down your cheek.
I was helpless, not knowing what to do. But I knew I couldn't leave you. Amidst the chaos, I held onto contentment in that momentary wilderness. I promised I would. Always. So I just sat there, held you, and, as you instructed, just loved you.

WANDERLUST

I've climbed peaks higher than the Himalayas. I've swum in oceans bluer and deeper than the Mediterranean. I've walked distances longer than the Great Wall of China. I may not have traveled the world and seen all its wonders and beauty yet, but you've already fulfilled all its greatest sights. I imagine the world is a beautiful place. And I always travel it with thoughts of you, experiencing a world I only want to see with you.

ASHES

We were moths to a flame. Enticed by its warmth, we surrendered to it and burned to ashes. Yet we survived. From ashes, we rose, and to ashes we'll one day return. For there is a fire which seems extinguished, but beneath the ashes the heat's still felt. If our love is to be a light, if it's to be our morning sun, our fire at night, we must learn to endure the burning of our hearts.

INFINITY

We were two individuals searching for that special one to make sense of our lives. We found each other and then a million little moments plus a thousand expressions of love formed an equation equaling infinity. The days. The nights. The good. The bad. The present. The future. The dreams. The fears. The magic. The madness. Trails we paved. Love we made. Apart, and neither world is defined. Together, everything makes more sense. With you. To infinity.

SENTIMENTAL EYES

Things that make me long for you:
Bora Bora
Hammocks
Dark colored fingernails
Women in cowboy boots
Lingerie
Mountains and valleys
Oceans and coasts
Globes
Pink Skies
Cookie Monster
Penguins
Christmas lights
Kissing couples
Flying W at Wrigley
Red roses
Lit candles
Pillows and blankets piled on a bed
Rain outside windows
Sunrises and sunsets

The moon and the stars and the airplanes that fly in between
Blank canvases
Filled wine glasses
Empty tequila bottles
My reflection

INTOXICATED

Moments after we've downed the tequila. Moments before lighting the candles. Moments when my heart beats rapidly as I undress you and you undress me. Moments when I touch you and ask, "Right there, Baby?" Moments before the ecstasy, after the fulfillment. Moments when words and actions aren't enough, when the only expression is the silence we interpret in each other's eyes. All these moments I drink to, waiting for them again every morning, day, and night.

A-MAZE

My father left me when I was young. I built a wall of insecurity. Girls rejected me because I was poor—another wall erected. My mother ignored me when I needed her the most. Another wall. For so long, walls confined me. But then you walked in. You loved me enough and made it through—not by trying to figure me out, but by knocking all the walls down. Sweetheart, I didn't find you. You found me.

THE FOUR ROOMS

The four seasons show me there is an appointed time for everything. The four elements reveal to me the universe and how it brings us together. The four winds announce there's nowhere I can go where I don't feel you. Then there's my heart, made up of the four rooms you inhabit. Some may have built it; others may have occupied it. But only you made it feel like home. You showed me the meaning of refuge.

Room I – The Physical

Your body is divine. Admiring it was a religion. With simple gazes I undressed you, made love to you a thousand times. And a thousand times I climaxed, grateful each time. Your tantalizing gait captivated me. Your stride left heaven's trail in its wake. I followed. When I reached you and touched you, I'd fall to my knees. Watching you dress was devotion, but nothing brought me to my knees quicker than seeing your splendid, naked figure.

Room II – The Intellectual

Though I consider you the most beautiful woman I've ever laid eyes on, you were always more to me than just looks. Though your style was fly, it was your mind that made my soul take flight. You always challenged me. You undressed my thoughts, made love to my conscience. In those moments, I fell deeper for you. In those moments, my love found its depth as your mind descended into mine and our souls became one.

Room III – The Emotional

You made it easy to share some of my most intimate secrets. In the midst of my fears, you were my comforter, and held me when I cried like a child. Many have passed through my heart—maybe others will again—but I will never be vulnerable with anyone the way I was with you. For you are the only one to ever make me feel that I could be strongest when I didn't have to be.

Room IV – The Spiritual

Faith never failed. Hope never left. Love never surrendered. I met you in the temporal; feeling as if I had always walked with you in the eternal. On life's journey, I've been emptied and filled. And throughout, it's you who's accompanied me every mile of the journey. As a child I prayed for you. As a man I found you. And if ever I'm lost again, it's God's face I'll seek, for finding Him I'll find you.

BROWN EYES

Beauty is measured in tones. Some love blue, others green. For me, beauty is found in her beautiful brown eyes, the ones that are more mystery than transparent, whose profoundness draw me in the way the moon draws tides. I can lose myself in them and never find my way back. Those beautiful brown eyes, deep in color, as strong as the one who unveils them, and able to hold me more tightly than arms ever could.

THE ARTIST

From our first interaction, I realized what I was, yet envisioned what I could be. I showed you trauma, but you saw triumph. You looked into my sad eyes and what you saw reflected in your sparkling, ethereal eyes. I was a mystery, a white canvas washed in black. In one stroke there was light; in another, there was love. After completing your masterpiece, you found what was lost, and I lost what I had been hiding.

AIRPLANES

Come fly with me. Let's fly, let's fly away. We'll take off, fly high, and soar above it all. Ground beneath our feet, wind behind our back, we'll soar into the clear blue sky until skies turn dark. To those beneath, we'll be nothing more than blinking lights, and to us, city lights will be our guiding stars. We'll wrap ourselves up in the clouds, dream with eyes open of the destinations awaiting. The world is ours.

FROM...TO

From secret gardens
To open fields
From drowning in the shallow
To swimming in the deep
From crying in your absence
To laughing in your presence
From "Baby, I wish you here."
To "Beautiful, I'm home."
From straight tequila shots by ourselves
To sipping and toasting margaritas with family
From singing alone
To "May I have this dance?"
From *Purple Rain*
To *Let's Go Crazy*
From we started at the bottom
To now we're at the top

LIFE SENTENCE

Blessed are we, beloved, who, despite the trials of life, remained steadfast in our commitment. Loving was never meant to be easy, yet we weathered the storm and withstood the fire. With remembrance came madness and with distance came closeness. Our faith stood trial, our hope endured detention, while our love faced execution. Through it all, we survived; through the suffering, we found new depths to what bound us together. There's nothing left to prove to anyone.

THE PLACES YOU TAKE ME

You make every day the best day. To paradise, you take me away.
Whatever the path, wherever it goes, promise you'll keep me close.
Whether soaring toward heaven or descending toward hell, in your comfort, I'll dwell.
Baby, you make me move mountains.
With you I ride the wind and let go of my cares.
You're my only wonder, for nothing compares.
The beauty, the bliss, you're my pleasure, my peace.
Oh, the places you take me!

MOURNING DOVE

Mourning dove, you who take flight each morning, whose gentle coos are heard across the winds. You whose song still echoes across time reminding me of the hour when the rest of the world stopped along the wooded trail, where my lips met hers for the very first time; carry with you my longing after this sleepless night and under the rising sun sit outside her window. And with your song remind her of my undying love.

UNIVERSE MOMENTS

The universe will always remind you. You will look and see our love reflected in things we found pleasure in. You will listen and hear the echoes of moments in which we both laughed and lived. In those moments, you will smile, and say to yourself, "I've lived this before." And somewhere, I'll be smiling too, knowing that the universe is signaling me back to you, that in the distance your heart still beats synchronously with mine.

NIGHTS OF WINE AND ROSES

The bottle uncorked
You serve me
Half-filled glasses
Water-filled vases
Red, blooming roses
The lights turned off
Candles lit
Fire burning
Incandescent light
You get comfortable
Your eyes watch
Dark, painted toenails, soft, supple breasts
Mmm!
"Can I have some more?"
I serve you
We sip
Red roses watch
Wine lips whisper, "You're so beautiful."

Intoxication and delirium set in
Roses flourish in water
Wine in the mouth
Passion in each other
And love in our home

LIT

We undress. Body on body, temperature rising. Smoke fills the room. I lay you down, wet with sweat and aflame with desire. We play with fire, wanting to burn. The friction from my fingers traces your skin; the spark of my lips kissing your curves stokes the flames until the bed combusts. My mouth navigates your body until I find my dripping well. I drink. Lit. Extinguished. Candles burn out; still, we glow like embers amongst ashes.

THE MOST DANGEROUS

We stand between a problem and a solution. We are one and you are the other. Questions arise inside me while you hold the answer, one you don't fully embrace. You teeter between the world we made and the world you feel you owe. And so here I am, between war and peace with my heart, in the hands of the most dangerous person: someone that doesn't love me, but also who doesn't want to lose me.

WARFARE

Night falls and the warfare begins.
Mind versus heart, the battle wages within.
The maddening mind is a gun that shatters the silence,
But the heroic heart conquers all thoughts of defiance.
A soldier of light armed with weapons of faith,
hope, and love.
Up the steep, rugged mountain, I climb, seeking
peace above all.
Embrace the struggle and fight for us; I will never stop.
Brave hearts will conquer, for our love waits at the top.

TAKING THE L

I'll never lose again because I'll never play again. I had but one heart left to give, and I gave it to you. Ergo: no more love to bestow. Though defeated, I walk away satisfied, having left a queen, knowing my love didn't just crucify you; it also crowned you. I'm sure you'll love again and live again, but you'll never find a love like mine again. Maybe yours is the biggest loss. I pray it's not.

FALLING TOWARD YOU

Love is a steep mountain I climb. I am weakened by every step I take, yet strengthened by the sight of what awaits. An irony of love, I suppose, that the more I fall, the more I find myself looking up. And the more I look up, the more reasons I find to love you. Every thought brings me closer to you as I fall between the empty cracks once filled by you, always falling toward you.

LOVER'S PRAYER

Heavenly Father, who art in heaven, I pray that love is more than enough, be it my love for her, her love for me, or your love for us. I pray if not me, then you. May you bring her someone who treats her the way you created her—beautiful and remarkable. But if I am the chosen one, then give me the wisdom to love her the same way you do, unconditionally and without blame. Amen.

SOLITUDE AND ME

Solitude: I know it's painful, but I promise I'm working for your good.
Me: I love her. So why does it hurt?
Solitude: Do you love the sun?
Me: Yes.
Solitude: You must also love the rain.
Me: Should I fear you?
Solitude: Fear loneliness. It brings poverty. But I bring you truth. That makes you rich.
Me: How long will you stay?
Solitude: Until you find your way back to her, and she takes my place.

SILENCE

There is silence that exists after the music has stopped and I'm left wondering, silence between thinking of the perfect words to text and hitting send, silence after a message is met with no reply, silence behind the smile of seeing couples laughing, silence after kissing an unwanted lover goodnight, silence after I've closed my eyes and whispered, "I still love you." But there is no more penetrating silence than when you've prayed and God says nothing.

THE UNKNOWN

How do I forget you? How do I know if all of this was real? Did I choose love? Did love choose me? What keeps me drawn to you? Your mind? Your heart? Why does love weaken the strong? Is love supposed to hurt? Do you miss me as much as I miss you? How many questions race through your mind? What are they? Same as mine? Which is scarier—the unknown? Or the truth being revealed?

THE WRITER

I am a writer with no words. Where do I find the perfect phrase when every word has been perfected by you? You are my muse. You are the wonder that precedes every story. I am a poet, yet have no rhyme. You are the lyric, yet have no music. I could write a prayer but, without you, it couldn't reach heaven. For I am a writer holding a pen, the ink of which flows through you.

HALO

I slept and found an angel in my dream. It blinded me with its bright halo and said to me as it wiped away my tears, "Don't be ashamed. If not for your tears, your flower would wither and die." Then I saw you sitting by a pond. "And if not for her tears, I wouldn't have come," the angel continued. As the halo glowed brighter, I saw myself immersed in the pond, drowning, yet still breathing.

REFLECTIONS AND ECHOES

Looking in the mirror, I don't see who I am, but rather who I was, who I still wish I could be in this life with you. Talking to myself, I don't hear my voice, but rather a soul being sung to. Emptiness and sadness are filled and made better with reflections of your smile, echoes of your words. Distance might blur the reflections, and time may silence the echoes, but the truths they carry always persist.

YOU, ME, AND DON JULIO

"One more?"
"One more."
With every shot, I feel you getting closer.
"Haha!" A nickname you used to call me triggers laughter.
The puzzled bartender looks over as he grabs the bottle off the shelf.
"Just know that when the love is real, pleasure can be found even in sadness."
"Your shot."
"Leave the bottle, please," I instruct. I clutch the over-filled glass.
"To you, my love…despite the time and distance, you sit right next to me."

WONDERLAND

Every day, I wonder if you still embrace our struggle. I wonder if simple and little things remind you of me. I wonder if you still play music, drawing me nigh to you. Every night, I wonder if you are having a glass of wine, thirsting for me as I still thirst for you. After I say a prayer for you, I wonder if you've done the same, and afterwards still utter the words, "Goodnight, my love."

NIGHT ROUTINE

I lay me down and close my eyes. I try to sleep, but to no avail. The night calls. Solitude beckons. I walk outside and go for a stroll, wondering as I step to the beat of my heart, to where you are. Stars are invisible; through rolling clouds, the moon struggles to be seen. Night doesn't cover our fears; it brings them to light. And so I stop, and pray, "God, may your light shine brighter."

LONGING TO DREAM

Nights are filled with dreams of you. I'm so tired of sleeping, but not tired of dreaming. If it's the only place I can have you, then I'll welcome every night just to see your face and hear your voice. Dreaming is my escape, like planting roses in a secret garden. You are a vision beneath closed eyelids, a sun in the wee hours of the night. And when morning comes, I awake, longing to dream again.

THE UNFADING ROSE

Her petals are bright. In darkness, her light is unveiled.
Her radiance is beautiful. In shadows, her beauty is remembered.
Her fragrance is sweet. In storms, her scent is alluring.
In the winter cold, she blooms. In the summer heat, she flourishes.
Time passes. Seasons change. Distance becomes greater, and I continue carrying my unfading rose.
And loving her, when I feel her thorns, I clutch her even closer, because that is where my love is revealed.

BETWEEN WISH YOU WELL AND WISH YOU WERE HERE

How to move on without looking back? Where do I find the good in goodbye? There's no looking forward without looking back. And, looking back, the desire remains to go back to where I once was. How do I wish you the best when together we were the best? I knew moving on would be difficult, but after having walked miles with you, moving on alone seems impossible. If we never meet again, I wish you love.

DARK SIDE OF THE MOON

Your love brought me to the other side of the moon. What once felt like Eden now feels like hell. Where once there was light, it's now dark. I sit alone with my thoughts. In the cold air, I long for your warm caress. Hungry and thirsty, I crave your mouth. The next time you see a full moon, please smile for me, pretty eyes, because from where I sit, you'll be the only light I'll see.

THE DARK PLACE

It's perhaps the darkest place, a place where devils reside; a place where all light is pulled in by fear. There is no safe bridge to cross and no one to guide you. It is a place where you must walk alone, because no one else understands; no one else can make sense of what you feel. One voice fights the other, and the one screaming loudest wins. Within the walls of your mind, you are trapped.

DYING TO LIVE

Autumn is here. You are the tree. I am the leaf. I will hold on until I can't hold on anymore. Even if I must die in the process, I will love you, for you're not just someone worth fighting for; you're also someone worth dying for. So I dream. I hope. I wish. Everything I do leads me to death. Because to love—to live, in fact—is to learn how to be okay with dying.

A BEAUTIFUL MESS

I still go crazy for you. In the comfort of my white, padded room, you adorn my walls. Hope may come in different forms but, to a madman, love comes by one: insanity. To this day, people don't really know who I am, how messed up I really am because of the distorted reality I live in, the far-reaching fantasy I envision. To me, it's better than the alternative. After all, what's the beauty in being normal?

BULLET HOLES

My heart's shot. I bleed. I never saw it coming. Even if I had, there's nothing I could've done. I held the gun, but you pulled the trigger. Though my soul was Teflon, your goodbye still pierced. BANG! It hit me. Silent. Slow. Fragile. I lost consciousness. Violently, I played. Violently, I lost. And only now I realize that the deepest of wounds are not the ones that people see but the ones that we carry inside.

KARMA

If ever I played the game of love unfairly, cheating another, it is I who now loses. If ever I plucked a flower just for its beauty, I'd replant it just to have my rose blossom again. If, in all my unconscious years and foolish ways, I hurt anyone, it is I who is now broken. If I could, I'd take back every false "I love you" to regain my true love, and tell her, "I'm sorry."

CHECKMATE

I was armed with reason, but you disarmed me with love. You were my Queen. I was your King, confident that I could see life coming several moves ahead. But the game required sacrifice, and I failed to make it. That was the difference. You said you needed a man who loved you enough not to run away. My running was pointless. From the beginning, you had me pinned. From the beginning, you held me captive. Checkmate.

THE OVERTHINKER

I want to call you. I don't. I want to run to you. I can't. When my mind turns on, my heart turns off. I try to reason with love. Why? Does love not have its own reasons for being? My emotions, feelings, and words are all subject to this prison, but the truth always sets free and there's nothing truer than *you're the one*. I promise—however much I overthink, that is how much I'll overlove.

SONNET LXXVII

Look at the sky. Now, look inside your heart. You will see that the beginning is not the beginning; the end is not the end. I loved you before I met you. In the early morning, my heart waited for you. Under the midday sun, it loved you. Come midnight, love kept my world aglow. Whether veiled in darkness or glorified in light, because our love was born in eternity, time will never kill what is ours.

THE OTHER FOUR

Things I close my eyes to, but the other senses still don't let me forget:
Mourning doves
Peony and Blush Suede perfume
Pumpkin spice
Peppermint gum
Chocolate chip cookies
Tajin rimmed margaritas
Cold brew with caramel
Whitney and Mariah
Frank Sinatra
Luis Miguel
Scent of a rose
Waves crashing on beach
"Hey!" "Hi!"
"Go, Cubs, Go"
Mosquito bites
Old-fashioned (with Maker's)
Warm buzz on chilly nights

Cold mornings
Thunderstorms
Wet grass under bare feet
My lover's prayer

STILL IN LOVE

Between shadow and soul, I still love you.
Between my here and your there, I still love you.
Between heaven and hell, I still love you.
Between the known and the unknown, I still love you.
Between January and December, I still love you.
Between the breaking and the healing, I still love you.
Between ignorance and reason, I still love you.
Between your life and beyond my death, I'll love you
till the end of time.

TO SEE YOU AGAIN

Can I see you again? Even if for one brief moment. Though I can't have you, can I see you and embrace the memory of what once was, briefly bringing to life what could've been? Can I see you and fill this void, even if for just one second? Can I see you and light this candle inside, feel the burn of desire? Can I see you again? Because I once could see, but now I'm blind.

THE POET'S CURSE

I write, yet who'll read my words if not you?
You are the water showering the concrete from
which I grew.
You are my muse, the refreshing fountain from
which my lyrics flow.
Holding on is hard, but even harder is letting go.
I write, yet who'll feel my heart?
For my life is worthless when we are apart.
The moon turns dark, the sun turns cold.
I sleep in the flesh; I dream of my soul.

NEVER A NIGHT

There are nights when I cry so hard my body aches, when the screams inside my head deafen all thoughts of moving on without you. There are also nights when I lie on my bed smiling peacefully, hoping and praying life is treating you well, thinking that everything happened just like it was supposed to. Then there are nights when I feel nothing at all. But there's never ever a night that you don't cross my mind.

COUNTERFEIT

They say the right things, but it feels so wrong. You are the truth.
They walk alongside me, but I can't move forward. You are the journey.
They sleep with me, but it's still you I dream of. You are the awakening.
The morning comes, yet the night still lingers. You are the sun.
In my loneliness, there are emotions that feel real, but I know they will eventually lead to death, because you are my life.

SONG CRY

I smile during the day, but come night, I sometimes cry. Some days, sadness takes on the shape of clouds, and I pray that it rains so that the rain and my tears become indistinguishable to others. But in between the drops, I hear your goodbye. The thunder then rolls. Or is it my heart? Can you hear it? Can you feel the tears? Can you feel the rain? It beats for you. I cry for you.

CRY HARD, LAUGH HARDER

I cried for you, but damn if I didn't also laugh with you. Your sarcasm, your impressions, your dirty mouth—I still laugh thinking about it all. Whether alone or in a crowd, hilarity ensues thinking about the playful things we did, the ignorant people we made fun of. Laughter made you lovable. Now it's that same laughter that makes life livable. Perhaps laughter's not just good medicine; after the tears, maybe it's also the best prayer.

FOREVER YOURS

Forever yours, even if you no longer dream of me,
Even if you no longer see days and nights alongside me.
Forever yours, even if, in another's arms, you find
what you seek
If the way I kissed, the way we made love, you no
longer speak
Forever yours, even if you walk alongside another
And new worlds and horizons he helps you discover
Forever yours, forever mine
One day, you and I, all in due time.

SEPARATE LIVES

You'll go your way and I'll go mine. And nothing will ever be the same. We'll look at photos and see ghosts. We'll hear echoes, but they'll be quieted. We'll walk paths, but they'll lead nowhere. We'll see the moonlight, but it'll be as dark and as void as the sky confining it. My heart will remain your home, but you'll no longer inhabit it. I'll go, and you'll go, and my love will go with you.

THE OTHER SIDE OF SILENCE

On the other side of silence, I hear our playlist. I hear my dedication to you: *Contigo en la distancia amada mía estoy*… I hear LANY: *Ain't never felt this way… I love you, Babe, so bad, so bad.* I hear Frank Sinatra in a jazz lounge crooning for us: *Come fly with me*… On the other side of silence, I hear my songbird singing my favorite lyrics of all: *My Love, can I say something crazy?*

LOVE TRAGEDY

Chapter I - Him

He walked by her today. She was as beautiful as he remembered her last. He asked how her new relationship was going. She smiled graciously and said, “Fine.” It hurt him to look at her. He almost broke. He feigned a smile and told her he missed her. She remained quiet, just offered him a friendly and merciful hug. “I love you so bad,” his words stayed trapped inside. He went home and cried. He lost her.

Chapter II - Her

She walked by him today. He was still her person and still would’ve chosen him. She wondered if he still cared. She asked how life was treating him; he said, “Okay.” He smiled tenderly. She could barely look at him without breaking yet found enough strength to smile back. “I miss you so much,” she wished he could’ve made sense of her thoughts. She held him one last time before going home to cry. She lost him.

Chapter III - The End

The saddened moon held their words and gazes but no longer shone because of the eclipse inside both their hearts. The grieving rainbow never again appeared because they couldn't withstand the rain. Between their hearts and minds existed a cold darkness that pulled them in because they failed acknowledging the truth within: a love like theirs only happened once. What might have been never became because they died choking on words they refused to speak. They lost.

CANTINA TEARS

The tequila is served. As I sip, I look over and observe a man and woman talking frantically in the corner booth.

"Another?" the bartender asks.

I slide the shot glass to the edge of the bar. Maybe it's generosity, maybe it's pity, but he pours me a double.

I glance over and notice the woman now sitting alone, crying. We stare intently at each other. Her tears call to me. I raise my glass to her.

MEET ME AT FOREVER

Meet me somewhere where words are not enough to
express my love for you.
Meet me somewhere where time is unconstrained,
where the smiles outlast the tears.
Meet me somewhere where I can kiss you and make
up for all our lost time.
Meet me somewhere where *I miss you*, *I need you* is
displaced by *I'll never leave you*.
Meet me somewhere where I can look at you,
reflecting this truth: I never stopped loving you.

TILL DEATH DO US PART

I, this flawed and imperfect man, take you, my beloved, to be my lady. Forever. Though we live apart, you'll die with me. I'll hold you and you'll join and share with me in all that's to come. Through the best of times, through the worst of times, I'll be yours and you'll be mine. Even from afar, I will be your biggest fan, your audience of one. In joy, in sorrow, till death do us part.

REVERENCE

I followed you to church. From the back pew, I sat and watched you. Your presence added majesty to the room. As requested, everyone closed their eyes, bowed their heads. All but me. My eyes stayed on you. God knew my heart. He knew the incense inside it still burned for you, for we were our own religion. And so, I wondered, what did you pray? "God, help me forget," or, "God, bring him back to me"?

ONE MORE NIGHT

Everything changed for me that one night. I've tried forgetting you, even prayed, "God, show me a way." But He just shows me my heart, the place in which you still live and still look as enchanting as you did when I first saw you. Since that night, I've seen a hundred moons and counted millions of stars, and I'd trade them all for one more night with you, to embrace you—and maybe change everything. Again.

MY ONE DAY

I believed you were my one day. After every heartbreak, I never stopped believing that we'd eventually meet. But then life interfered, and again I was left giving it my all while you gave none. And just when I thought that you'd gotten it right where others had gotten it wrong, you unfortunately failed me too. You changed the narrative. Briefly. Now I return to the story of my life, still hoping for my one day's arrival.

YOU KNOW

This is where I leave you. With a smile. Because my smile says so much—but you already know that. You know it says how important you were to me. You know that it holds back the tears that are likely to spill over if I open my mouth to speak. You know it rights the wrongs and softens the hurt. My smile says I'll forever love you, but you know that. I hope you always knew.

A LETTER TO MYSELF

Dear Me,

I'm sorry for allowing the hurt to persist as long as it did, for not knowing what was good for you. Thank you because through the first crush, first heartbreak and now the first breakdown, you've never let go. You always bounce back stronger and wiser. Now I want you to love yourself the same way you loved her, intimately and fearlessly, because no one deserves that kind of love more than you.

Love,
Me

FLY THE W

Love isn't a losing game. We, through the choices we make, are left holding losing hands. But love is perfect. It never loses. Winners are those who, with tears in their eyes, make others smile and, while discouraged, still encourage others. Winners are those who still hold onto hope at 3 a.m. because they know its love's call that keeps them awake. They know if they can hold on just a little longer, they will eventually win.

IN THE END

When I met you, I dove in with furor and anticipation. Once in the water, love navigated me toward the depths of your spirit, body, and mind. When I realized how far from the shallow I'd swum, it was too late. I don't know if I loved you too much or if I didn't love you enough. In the end, I do know I'll never love the same again. In the end, you were worth the drowning.

My gratitude could never be contained to just seventy-seven words. First, and above all, I would like to thank God for the resilient heart I carry inside. Despite the breaking, it always bounces back, bringing back a needed blessing.

I would like to thank everyone I love and have loved, as well as all who have loved me in return. Love has taken me to the heights of heaven and other times to the depths of hell. But on every journey, I am grateful to have always been taken somewhere and taught lessons that never would have been learned if I had not chosen to take a risk by opening my heart to you.

And finally, I want to thank all those who took a chance in reading my words. Your time and attention are greatly appreciated. A life worth living is measured in many ways. One way is in the way we encounter others. Through this book, I'm grateful our paths crossed. Till we meet again, faith, hope and love.

7OVE ETERNA7

www.ingramcontent.com/pod-product-compliance
Lightning Source LLC
LaVergne TN
LVHW012111160826
845678LV00014B/3042

* 9 7 9 8 4 8 9 4 1 3 7 3 2 *